A Running Back Can't Always Rush

by Nate LeBoutillier

illustrated by Jorge Santillan

Sports Illustrated KIDS

STONE ARCH BOOKS

a capstone imprint

Sports Illustrated KIDS *A Running Back Can't Always Rush*
is published by Stone Arch Books – A Capstone Imprint
151 Good Counsel Drive, P.O. Box 669
Mankato, Minnesota 56002
www.capstonepub.com

Art Director and Designer: Bob Lentz
Creative Director: Heather Kindseth
Production Specialist: Michelle Biedscheid

Timeline photo credits: Library of Congress (top right);
Shutterstock/dubassy (middle left), Trinacria Photo (top
left); Sports Illustrated/Heinz Kluetmeier (bottom right),
Peter Read Miller (bottom left).

Library of Congress Cataloging-in-Publication Data is
available on the Library of Congress website.
ISBN: 978-1-4342-2055-4 (library binding)
ISBN: 978-1-4342-2805-5 (paperback)

Summary: Danny loves to use his super speed all the time,
especially on the football field, but going too fast causes him
some big problems.

Printed in the United States of America in Stevens Point, Wisconsin.
032010   005741WZF10

TABLE of CONTENTS

VICTORY
SCHOOL
SUPERSTARS

DANNY

CARMEN

DANNY

KENZIE

JOSH

ALICIA

TYLER

Never Look Back

My mind races. It is the final quarter of today's big game. I am lined up in the backfield, and I am thinking ahead. In a couple seconds, Ray, the quarterback, will hand the football to me. I'm Danny, the running back. It's my job to run with the ball.

I'm supposed to go left, but I see two players from the other side move to that spot. They are linebackers, and their job is to tackle me. But I have a plan.

"Hut, hut!" says Ray.

Every player starts to move. The players are like a school of very big fish.

Ray hands off the football to me. I fake left, then spin back around to the right. No one is in the way. I start to speed. My legs are chugging. My feet barely touch the ground. You see, I have super speed. I was born with it.

I look back. A player leaps to tackle me.
I push myself even faster! He grabs at the air
behind me and lands with an "Oof!"

I zip into the end zone. I don't want to stop running because it feels so good. But when you score a touchdown, the play is over.

"Danny," says Coach Pushner, "nice play, but I want you to remember something."

"What's that?" I ask.

Coach Pushner says, "Never look back, Danny. Do you think cheetahs look back? Looking back only slows you down."

"Okay, Coach," I say.

After the game, Coach tells us to huddle up. "Good game, guys," he says. "But tomorrow's game will be even tougher. The Comets are hard to stop."

I can't wait for the game against the Comets. It will be the first time I will get to play against our big rival.

But every game with the Superstars is exciting. All my classmates at the Victory School for Super Athletes have amazing abilities, like my super speed. Playing on this team is like going on a fun vacation. It's new, it's exciting, and there are lots of chances for great photos!

Too Fast

Later that evening, my family sits at the dinner table. We're having one of my favorite meals: tomato soup, grilled cheese sandwiches, and peas. I gobble everything quickly.

My twin sister, Alicia, is telling us all what happened in cheerleading practice. Two guys with super strength had a contest to see who could lift their partners the longest.

"It might sound like a fun contest," says Alicia, "but we did not appreciate being stuck in the air for over an hour."

We all laugh. It seems like kids at Victory are always competing!

"Can I be excused?" I ask. "Some of the guys are meeting at the park for a game before it gets dark."

"Did you even chew your food before swallowing?" asks Dad.

"Yep," I say. "Can I go now? I want to go play before it gets dark. Please? Can I?"

My dad looks at my mom.

"Did you do your chores?" asks Mom.

"I'll do them before I go," I say. "Right away."

"Okay," says Mom.

I hurry to the back porch. In a flash, I take the garbage out. Then I refill the food dish for my dog, Thunderbolt. Within seconds, I am sprinting toward the park.

Ray spots me. "Hey, Danny!" he yells. Ray, of course, has a powerful arm. He can throw the football a mile. He launches the football into the air like a rocket, way past me. I dash after it and nab it.

Ray is impressed. "Danny, you're the fastest kid I've ever seen," he says.

We start our game, but after just a few minutes, I have to quit. "Sorry guys, I'm not feeling too great," I say. "I'm going home."

I start trotting home. My super speed doesn't do me any good at the moment.

Feeling Bad

On the way home, I walk past my classmate Kenzie's house. Kenzie is a gymnast with super strength. She is lifting her family's minivan off the ground with one hand while her father works underneath it. Her strength comes in really handy sometimes.

"Hey, Danny," asks Kenzie. "What's wrong?"

"Aw, nothing. I've just got a little stomachache," I say. "I guess I ate my dinner too fast."

"Maybe you should slow down," Kenzie teases. Just for fun, she grabs a nearby picnic table with her free hand and starts lifting it like a dumbbell.

"Maybe I should. See ya," I say. I walk away, holding my belly.

As I get closer to home, I spot my sister Alicia. She is dragging a garbage bag to the curb. "You forgot one," she says. I can tell she isn't happy.

"Sorry," I say as Alicia tugs the bag past me.

Inside the house, my father is holding Thunderbolt like a baby and scratching his belly. Thunderbolt whines like a rusty wheel.

"What's wrong with him?" I ask.

"He ate too much," says Dad. "Someone overfilled his food dish."

Now other parts of me, along with my stomach, feel bad, too.

You're Suspended

Students at Victory don't just play sports. They have classes like regular kids, too. I like math. Sometimes, the teacher, Ms. Best, lets the students race to see who can finish problems first. I finish ahead of the rest today.

Ms. Best looks over my work. "Danny, you forgot a whole row!" she says. "And your handwriting is a mess. Speed can make you sloppy."

Rats, I think.

In band class, I play the bass drum. When all the instruments play together, I get excited, and I hit the drum too fast. "Slow down, Danny!" says my band teacher. "This is a piece of music, not a race."

Whoops, I think.

In art class, we're making sculptures out of popsicle sticks. My tower falls because I don't wait long enough for the glue to dry.

Aw, man, I think.

Later I get some bad news from Coach Pushner, who is also my English teacher.

"You forgot to write sentences from your spelling words," says Coach Pushner. "What happened?"

I slap my palm against my forehead.

"I must have missed that part in the directions," I say.

"That's the third time this month that you didn't complete your assignment," says Coach Pushner. "I'm sorry, Danny, but that means you can't play in the game today. You're suspended."

His words tackle me just like a linebacker. I limp around the rest of the school day like I'm injured, even though I'm not.

At the game, I stand on the sidelines as my teammates throw, catch, run, and dive. Ray throws a touchdown at the end to give us the win. The team is happy. I try to be happy, too, and a part of me is. But I miss running fast on the field.

Some Good Advice

At home, I eat my dinner slowly, even though it's spaghetti, my favorite.

Mom asks, "What's wrong, Danny? Is something bothering you?"

Dad asks, "Did you lose the game today?"

Alicia asks, "What's with you? Spaghetti's your favorite."

Thunderbolt looks at me and tilts his head. It seems like everyone has questions for me tonight.

"I guess I'm just not that hungry," I say. "May I be excused?"

My parents excuse me from the table. Outside in the yard, I sit down under a tree for a long while, thinking slowly.

Kenzie walks by. She's giving her little sister a ride in a stroller. She stops and asks, "How was the game?"

"I didn't play," I say.

"Why not?" Kenzie asks.

I can't answer. I feel like crying. And I can't think of anything more embarrassing than crying in front of a girl.

"Do you feel like taking a walk?" Kenzie asks.

"Sure," I say.

We walk slowly and quietly because Kenzie's sister has fallen asleep.

"Coach told me to never look back," I say.

"That seems like good advice for football," says Kenzie. "But I don't think that would work all the time. Sometimes slow is better than fast. Sometimes you have to slow down."

"For me, slow is never better than fast. I like being fast," I say. "I don't want to be slow."

"Fast is good on the football field, but you don't play football all the time," says Kenzie. "A running back can't *always* rush. Sometimes you have to hold back. Think of what might happen if I used my super strength all the time."

"You'd probably crush that stroller!"
I say with a laugh. "And no one would
ever want to shake your hand."

"Or give me a hug," Kenzie says. "Imagine
the damage!"

After a while, I head home. I think I know what I have to do now.

That night, I take a bath, nice and slow. The water feels warm and bubbly. I do my homework and check it twice. I give Thunderbolt a belly rub for forty minutes.

I listen to Alicia practice a speech for class, and I don't look at the clock even once. In fact, for the next week, I take my time with almost everything.

Zoom!

The next game day finally arrives. I feel excited. Energy pumps through me. At breakfast, I am tempted to gobble my pancakes quickly. I take two big bites, but then I notice Alicia looking at me, shaking her head. I slow down.

At school, it's hard to focus. My mind is on nothing but the game.

I start whizzing through my math problems. Ms. Best walks by and points at my messy numbers. I erase them and write in new ones, slowly and neatly.

In the locker room before the game, I start to focus. I get my mind ready for the game.

"Hey, Danny," says Ray, "you sure look ready to go. I'm not used to seeing you so calm before you play."

"What do you mean?" I ask.

Ray grins. "Remember our last practice?" he asks. "You put your pants on backwards and your shoes on the wrong feet!"

I laugh. "How could I forget?"

Finally, it's game time! I'm so happy to be on the field, I can barely feel my body.

On the first play, Ray hands the ball off to me.

The defense rushes in. I know that the time to be patient is over. It's time to speed up.

Zoom! I am in the end zone again.

SUPERSTAR OF THE WEEK
Danny Gohl

When you're as fast as Danny Gohl, you never want to slow down. It was hard for Danny to control his speed, but he did it! That makes him our Superstar of the Week.

You had a tough week. What was the worst part?
I knew I needed to slow down. But asking me to slow down is like asking a turtle to speed up. I just couldn't do it. Worst of all, I was letting people down.

But you managed to get control over your speed. How did that feel?
Well, when I finally got to run fast, it felt better than ever! I felt unstoppable out there!

What do you like to do when you aren't playing football or going to school?
It isn't hard to guess. I just really like to run. Some of my friends are into video games, but I get bored staying in one spot. I have a lot more fun zooming around town.

With all that running, you must feel hungry all the time. What is your favorite snack?
I like a lot of different foods, but chips and salsa are my favorite!

GLOSSARY

abilities (uh-BIL-i-teez)—skills or powers

backfield (BAK-feeld)—the area on a football field behind the line where players line up for each play

competing (kuhm-PEET-ing)—trying hard to outdo others at a task, race, or contest

end zone (END ZOHN)—the last ten yards at either end of the field

linebackers (LINE-bak-ers)—players on the defending team who usually stand behind the line where players line up before each play

quarterback (KWOR-tur-back)—a player who passes the ball or hands it off to a runner

running back (RUHN-ing BAK)—a player who the quarterback hands off the ball to

suspended (suh-SPEND-ed)—punished by being stopped from taking part in an activity for a short while

tackle (TAK-uhl)—to knock or pull a person to the ground

touchdown (TUCH-doun)—when the ball is carried into the other team's end zone; it is worth six points.

FOOTBALL IN HISTORY

1869   Rutgers and Princeton Universities play the first official **football** game.

1876   Sports writer and football coach Walter Camp writes the first rules of football.

1905   Eighteen players die playing football. **President Teddy Roosevelt** calls for changes in the rules to make the game safer.

1920   Eleven teams form the American Professional Football Association. It later becomes the NFL.

1939   First NFL game is **televised**.

1967   The Green Bay Packers beat the Kansas City Chiefs in the first official Super Bowl.

1985   Led by fan favorites, Jim McMahon, **Walter Payton**, and William "The Refrigerator" Perry, the 1985 Chicago Bears team is one of the greatest NFL teams of all time.

2004   De La Salle High School of Concord, California is beat for the first time since 1992. They hold the national record for longest winning streak with 151 wins.

2010   NFL legends Jerry Rice and **Emmitt Smith** are voted into the Hall of Fame. Together, they hold twenty NFL records.

ABOUT THE AUTHOR

NATE LEBOUTILLIER

While growing up in southwestern Minnesota, Nate LeBoutillier read any sports books he could get his hands on. He now lives with his family in North Mankato, Minnesota. He began writing children's books in 2001 and has published many nonfiction titles. He also writes adult short fiction, novels, and screenplays. When not writing, Nate can be found playing with his kids, listening to music, or training for triathlons.

ABOUT THE ILLUSTRATOR

JORGE SANTILLAN

Jorge Santillan got his start illustrating in the children's sections of local newspapers. He opened his own illustration studio in 2005. His creative team specializes in books, comics, and children magazines. Jorge lives in Mendoza, Argentina, with his wife, Bety, and their four dogs, Fito, Caro, Angie, and Sammy.

VICTORY ★ SCHOOL SUPERSTARS

Read them ALL!

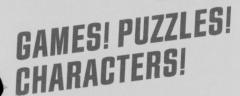